THE
CHALK BOX KID

By Clyde Robert Bulla

Illustrated by Thomas B. Allen

A STEPPING STONE BOOK

Random House New York

To Stephanie Spinner

Text copyright © 1987 by Clyde Robert Bulla. Illustrations copyright © 1987 by Thomas B. Allen. All rights reserved under International and Pan-American Copyright Conventions. Published in the United States by Random House, Inc., New York, and simultaneously in Canada by Random House of Canada Limited, Toronto.

Library of Congress Cataloging-in-Publication Data: Bulla, Clyde Robert. The chalk box kid. (A Stepping stone book) SUMMARY: Nine-year-old Gregory's house does not have room for a garden, but he creates a surprising and very different garden in an unusual place. [1. Artists—Fiction. 2. Imagination—Fiction. 3. Gardens—Fiction] I. Allen, Thomas B., ill. II. Title. PZ7.B912Cas 1987 [E] 87-4683 ISBN: 0-394-89102-3 (trade); 0-394-99102-8 (lib. bdg.)

Manufactured in the United States of Ameri·   5 6 7 8 9 10

Contents

1
The Room

Gregory heard the clock strike. It was an hour till midnight. His birthday would soon be over.

He went to the door and looked out into the street.

"Shut the door," said Aunt Grace.

"I thought I heard the car," he said.

"Gregory," said his aunt, "the cold air is coming in."

He shut the door. He went back and sat by her on the sofa. His tablet and paints and brushes were out on the table, but he didn't feel like painting. He sat there and tried to watch television with Aunt Grace.

It had been a long day. So far it was his very worst birthday.

He had wanted to go with Mother and Daddy. They were moving to another house, and he hadn't even seen it yet.

"If you go with us, you'll just get tired," Mother had said. "I want you to stay with Aunt Grace."

He had thought she didn't remember what day it was. He had told her, "I'm nine years old today."

"I know," she had said, "and I'm sorry we can't have a cake or a party. There's just no time. We have to finish moving."

But he kept thinking there would be *something* for his birthday.

He went to the door again. This time the car was there. Mother was getting out.

She came up to the door. She had on old

clothes, and she looked tired. "Hello, Grace," she said. "Thank you for keeping Gregory. Are you ready, Gregory?"

He picked up his tablet and paints and brushes, and he was ready.

They went out to the car. She sat up front with Daddy. Gregory got into the back.

They drove across the city. Gregory went to sleep.

When he woke up, they had stopped under a streetlight. The light shone on a house.

"Is this it?" he asked.

"This is it," said Daddy.

Daddy had lost his job at the factory. Now he had a different job. That was why they had had to move.

The house was small and it needed paint. It looked as if it had grown out of the sidewalk. There was no yard at all.

They went inside. Gregory saw boxes and papers. He saw bare walls.

"You'd better go to bed," said Mother.

"Where?" he asked.

She showed him a room. His bed was in it.

His chair and table were in it too.
　He asked, "Is it—is it mine?"
　"Do you like it?" she asked.
　"Oh, yes!" he said.

"It used to be a porch," she told him. "We had a wall put in, and the window."

So there *was* something for his birthday. There was something better than a cake or a party.

"Go to bed now," said Mother. She went out and left him there.

He sat on the bed and looked at the room. It was not very wide, but it was long. It was a big room for such a little house. He looked at the floor and the walls and the ceiling. He looked into every corner. This was what he had always wanted—a room of his own.

He heard a clock strike. His birthday was over, and it was the best birthday he had ever had!

2
Uncle Max

Gregory woke early. The day was coming in. He lay there and looked at the room that was all his.

By the bed was the box he and Mother had packed. His things were in it.

He got up and began to dig in the box. He found his old yellow robe and put it on.

His tablet and paints and brushes were on the

table where he had put them last night. Without making any noise, he went into the kitchen and brought back a cup of water. He sat down at his table and began to paint. The paper in his tablet was too small, but he painted a red house that wasn't bad. He painted a sunflower that was a little better.

Mother came to the door.

He asked her, "Do we have any thumbtacks?"

"What do you want with thumbtacks?" she asked.

"I want to put my pictures up," he said.

She brought him some tacks.

He put his pictures up on the wall. They looked good there, even if they were too small. Now the room looked like it was really his.

He and Mother and Daddy had breakfast.

"I'll make more coffee for Max," said Daddy.

Gregory asked, "Is Uncle Max coming here?"

"He is," said Daddy.

"Then I'm going out," said Gregory.

"Where?" asked Mother.

"Up the street," he said.

"I don't know—" said Mother.

"Oh, let him go," said Daddy. "He just wants to see the new neighborhood. Isn't that right, Gregory? Don't you want to see the new neighborhood?"

"Yes," said Gregory.

He went out. The air was cold, but it felt good. It felt like spring.

He walked up the street. It was Sunday morning, and not many people were out. He saw a grocery store. He saw a few places that looked like garages or small factories.

The next block got better. There were more houses and trees. In the block after that, he came to a school. It was the Dover Street School. Mother had told him about it. He would be going there.

He walked a few more blocks, and then he went home. His uncle Max was there.

Uncle Max was twenty. He had a red beard, and he played the guitar and made up songs. Most of the time he was out of work.

"Well!" he said in his loud voice. "Here comes the Great Gregory! Here comes the Paintbrush Kid!"

"Hello," said Gregory.

He went to his room. The door was open. There was another bed in the room. There was a guitar on the bed.

Mother called him into the kitchen. "Uncle Max will be with us for a while," she said. "He isn't working now. He needs a place to stay."

Gregory looked at her.

"It won't be so bad," she said.

"It's not my room," he said. "It's his."

"It's yours, too," she said.

But he knew how that would be.

"Why don't you like your uncle Max?" she asked.

"He thinks he's important," said Gregory.

"He is important," said Mother. "We all are."

"He thinks no one is important but him," said Gregory.

He went outside. There was concrete all around the house. Even the wall across the back was concrete. There was a gate in the wall. It was painted green—an ugly green.

He could hear Uncle Max playing the guitar, and he kicked the gate. He kicked it so hard that some of the paint fell off.

3
The New School

In the morning Mother and Daddy got ready for work. She cooked in a restaurant. He was a guard in a bank.

Mother asked Gregory, "Do you want your uncle to go with you to the new school?"

Gregory shook his head.

"Don't you want someone to help you get started?" she asked.

"No," he said. "I've done it before."

He went to school. He found the office. A woman there sent him to Room 3, and that was his room.

His teacher was Miss Perry. She said to the class, "We have a new boy in our room. His name is Gregory."

She asked what school he had come from.

"North Lake," he said.

"Is that here in the city?" she asked.

"Yes. It's a big school," he told her. "It's bigger than this."

He liked Miss Perry. He thought he was going to like Dover Street School. He began to learn the names of the boys and girls.

At noon a boy named Vance came up to him on the playground. Vance was the biggest boy in Room 3.

"Did you say you went to North Lake School?" he asked.

"Yes," said Gregory.

"What made you say it's a big school?" asked Vance.

Some other boys and girls had come by. They were listening.

"It *is* a big school," said Gregory.

"No, it isn't," said Vance. "I've been there, and it's not as big as this."

"It looks bigger," said Gregory.

"Well, it isn't," said Vance. "You like to brag, don't you?"

"I wasn't bragging," said Gregory. "I just said it was bigger. I didn't say it was better."

He stopped. No one was listening. Vance and the others had gone away.

After school he walked home alone. Uncle Max was there, watching television.

Gregory went into the room that was his and his uncle's. There were pictures on the walls that he had never seen before. They were big red and black posters of race cars. Gregory's pictures were nowhere in sight.

He went back to the front room. "Where are my pictures?" he asked.

The television was turned up loud. Uncle Max turned it down. "What did you say?"

"My *pictures,*" said Gregory. "Where are they?"

"They're still there," said his uncle.

"You put your posters over my pictures?" said Gregory.

"Don't you like my posters?" asked Uncle Max.

"No, I don't!" said Gregory.

"That's too bad," said Uncle Max, and he turned the television up again.

Gregory was angry. He wanted to go into the bedroom and tear down all his uncle's posters.

But that would only make things worse.

He went out back and tried to find something to do. He shook the gate in the wall. There was a wire that held it shut.

He began to work with the wire. He worked until it came loose. He opened the gate.

On the other side was part of a building. The building had burned. One room was left. It had three walls and no roof, and there were bricks all over the floor. It looked as if no one had been there for a long time.

Gregory went in. He walked through spider webs and dust.

He piled up some bricks and sat down on them. He leaned back and looked at the sky. It was peaceful here, and he began to feel better. He was not quite so angry now.

4
The Burned Building

In Room 3 there was a girl named Ivy. She was small, with long black hair. She was shy. When she talked, it wasn't much more than a whisper.

There was something wonderful about her. Gregory wasn't sure what it was, but it was there in her face and the way she held her head. It was in the pictures she made.

Three times a week they had art class in Room 3.

Once Gregory said to Ivy, "Your pictures are good."

She looked at a picture he had just made. It was a castle. He didn't much like it. He had wanted to put a flag on top, but he had made the castle too big. There was no room for the flag.

Ivy said nothing at all, but she touched the picture. He wasn't sure whether she liked it or not.

Since his first day, things hadn't gone very well for him at the new school. He hoped they would get better, but after a week they were about the same. He thought Miss Perry liked him. He didn't know about the others.

Things weren't going so well at home, either. Uncle Max was always there. He was always watching television. Or going *plink, plink, plink* on the guitar. Or sleeping in their room.

It was more his room than Gregory's, but now Gregory didn't mind so much. He had a place of his own. Every day after school he went out to the burned building.

"Can't you find somewhere else to play?" asked Mother. "You'll get all dirty out there."

"I'm cleaning it up," he said.

When he swept the floor, he found little pieces of something white. He showed one of them to Mother. "It looks like chalk," he said.

"It *is* chalk," she said.

A few days later she told him, "I found out about the burned building. The woman next door told me. It used to be a chalk factory. A man made chalk and tried to sell it to schools, but he didn't do very well. The place caught fire and burned, and the man just went away and left it."

Gregory kept sweeping up more chalk. One day he found two wooden boxes under a pile of bricks. They were packed with sticks of chalk.

The boxes were burned and broken. Some of the chalk was burned and broken, too, but some of it was clean and white.

The walls of the burned building were black from the fire. He tried making chalk pictures on them. He made a ship and an alligator.

Mother came to the gate and called him to dinner.

"Do you want to see what I made?" he asked.

"Some other time," she said. "Your dinner is getting cold."

5
A Party

Gregory's second week in the new school began with a party. It was for Ivy.

Gregory asked the teacher, "Is this her birthday?"

"Oh, I forgot to tell you," said Miss Perry. "You weren't here last month, so you don't know what happened."

There had been an art show, she told him. The whole school took part. There were more than five hundred pictures in the show.

"And who do you think won the grand prize?" she asked.

"Ivy!" he said.

"Yes, Ivy," said Miss Perry. "She won the blue ribbon. The art teacher and I wanted her to have a special prize. We got it yesterday, and we're giving it to her today. That's what the party is about."

The prize was on the teacher's desk. It was a package wrapped in gold paper.

The art teacher, Miss Cartright, came in. She made a speech about the art show. She called Ivy up to the front.

"All the school is proud of you," she said, and she gave Ivy the package.

Ivy held it in her hands, and then she said a strange thing. "Maybe this isn't for me."

"What do you mean?" asked Miss Cartright.

"I mean," Ivy said in her whispering voice, "there could be somebody better."

"We think you are the best," said Miss Cartright.

Ivy took the package to her seat.

"Aren't you going to see what it is?" asked Miss Perry.

Slowly Ivy took off the gold paper. There was something inside that looked like a big book. But it wasn't a book. It was a leather case.

Ivy opened it. She sat very still.

The other girls and boys were trying to see what was in the leather case.

"Do you want to pass it around?" asked Miss Cartright.

Ivy passed the case around. It came to Gregory. There were paints and brushes inside. There were pens and pencils. There was almost everything an artist could want, he thought.

That evening he told Mother about the party.

"That must have been fun," she said. "Do you like school?"

"It's all right," he said.

"Have you made any friends?"

"Well, no," he said. "There is this Vance in my room. He doesn't like me much. He has a lot of friends, and I don't think they like me either."

"It takes a while to get used to a new school," she said. "Don't worry about it."

"I don't," he said.

But he did worry sometimes. He didn't seem to belong in the new school. He wondered if he ever would.

6
Mr. Hiller

Mr. Hiller came to Room 3. He was a friend of Miss Perry's.

"Mr. Hiller works in a nursery," she said. "Who knows what a nursery is?"

One of the girls spoke up. "It's a room for a baby."

"That is one kind," said Miss Perry. "Mr. Hiller works in another kind. He works in a plant nursery. He sells plants and seeds, and he is here to tell us about them."

Mr. Hiller talked about gardens. As he talked he drew pictures on the blackboard. He drew a bunch of lettuce with curly leaves. He drew a round head of lettuce. "You can grow both kinds," he said.

He talked about radishes. "You can grow the ones that are round and red," he said, "or you can grow the long white ones." He drew a picture of each kind.

He talked about flowers. He drew a sweet pea vine on a pole.

"Next week," he said, "I'll bring some plants and seeds to school. There will be some for each of you. If you want to, you can have your own gardens."

That evening Gregory told Mother about Mr. Hiller. "I'm going to have a garden," he said.

"Gregory, I don't think you can," she said.

"Why not?" he asked.

"There's no place for one," she said.

He looked outside. There was concrete all around the house. He looked in the burned building. The floor there was concrete too.

Mother was right. He had no place for a garden.

He had wanted to plant all the things Mr. Hiller had drawn on the blackboard. The curly lettuce was what he liked best.

He took a piece of chalk and drew a bunch on the wall. It was not very good. He drew another one. That was better. He drew more bunches of curly lettuce. He drew a long row of them. They looked good in a row.

That was Friday. On Monday, Mr. Hiller came back to school. He brought plants and seeds. Girls and boys chose what they wanted. Ivy chose sweet pea seeds.

Gregory stayed in his seat.

Miss Perry asked him, "Don't you want any?"

"No, thank you," he said. "I already have a garden."

7
Gregory's Garden

Gregory's garden was in the burned building. It was in the room with three walls.

He had rubbed out the ship and the alligator he had drawn. They didn't belong in a garden.

He had made rows of vegetables across the walls. He had made sunflowers. He had put in poles with sweet peas on them.

He made a path. The path led to a pool. He put a toad by the pool.

"Come and see my garden," he said to Mother.

"You know I don't like that burned building," she said. "Can't you find a better place to play?"

"It isn't ugly now," he said. "I cleaned it up."

He asked his father, "Do you want to see my garden?"

"Are there any strawberries?" asked Daddy.

"I can put some in," said Gregory.

"You do that," said Daddy. "Put in lots of strawberries. When they are ripe, I'll come out and eat them with sugar and cream."

Gregory didn't ask Uncle Max to look at his garden. Uncle Max would only laugh.

At school the girls and boys talked about their gardens.

Miss Perry asked Gregory, "How is your garden?"

"All right," he said. Ivy was there, and he said to her, "I have poles with sweet peas on them."

Ivy said nothing. Miss Perry said, "That's nice. What else do you have?"

"Vegetables," he told her. "And I have a path to the pool."

She looked surprised. "Your garden must be big."

"It is," he said.

And he had plans to make it bigger.

He took the ladder out of the garage. He set it up in the garden room. When he was on the ladder, he could reach the top of the walls. Now he could have trees in his garden.

He made a pear tree and a walnut tree. He made vines to hang from the branches. He made birds' nests in the trees.

It rained one night, and he lay awake. *My garden will be gone,* he thought.

But it was not gone. Only a few vegetables were washed away.

He was almost late to school that morning. He told the teacher, "I was working in my garden. The rain washed out some of my lettuce."

"You work in your garden a lot, don't you?" said Miss Perry.

"Yes, I do," he said. "I may put in a fountain."

Vance was listening. At noon he asked Gregory, "So where is this garden with the fountain in it?"

"I don't have a fountain yet," said Gregory.

"You're always talking about your garden. Where is it?" asked Vance.

"Back of my house," said Gregory.

Afterward he saw some of the boys and girls with their heads together. They were looking at him and talking. He thought they were talking about him.

8
"Nothing At All"

When Gregory got home from school, he went straight to his garden. He was thinking about the fountain. The garden spread over three walls. He would have to take out something to make room for the fountain. But he liked to change things.

He started to the garage to get the ladder. He stopped. There were footsteps outside the gate.

Someone laughed. Someone went "Shh!"

The gate opened. Boys and girls came pushing in. They were all from Room 3.

Vance was the leader. He said, "We came to see your garden."

"Where is it?" asked one of the girls.

"*This* is it," said Vance.

"It's just a burned-out building," said someone else.

"Didn't I tell you?" said Vance. "It's nothing. It's nothing at all."

He turned and walked out. The others followed him. And the last one out was Ivy!

She looked back. She almost stopped. Then she was gone.

That night Gregory wasn't hungry. There was chocolate chip ice cream for dessert. It was his favorite, but he couldn't eat it.

Mother felt his forehead. "It feels hot. I think you should be in bed."

He went to bed. She sat with him.

"Gregory, what's wrong?" she asked.

He began to tell her. "Some of the others at school have gardens. I said I had one too."

"Why did you say that?" she asked.

"Because I do have one," he said. "It isn't like theirs, but it's a garden."

"The one you made in the burned building?" she asked.

"Yes. And after school they followed me home. They came in to look, and they said—"

"What did they say?"

"They said it was nothing at all. They thought I was just bragging."

"And you weren't bragging?"

"No, I wasn't. Maybe I was pretending—a little—but I wasn't bragging. They can think what they want to," he said. "I don't care!"

9
Ivy and Richard

But it was hard for him to go to school the next day. When he got there, he walked around the block before he went in. He was the last one in Room 3.

Miss Perry smiled at him. He didn't think she knew. But the others did. He could feel them looking at him.

Ivy sat up front. Miss Perry spoke to her. "Are

you going to make us a picture today?"

Ivy had brought her leather case to school. She didn't answer Miss Perry. She stood up and came straight to Gregory. She put the case down on his desk and went back to her seat.

The room was still.

Miss Perry looked puzzled. She asked, "Do you want Gregory to use your paints and brushes?"

"They're not mine," said Ivy.

"Of course they are," said Miss Perry.

"No," said Ivy. "They're Gregory's."

"How could they be Gregory's?" asked Miss Perry.

"Because—because his pictures are better than mine," said Ivy. "I saw them on the walls. And they're better!"

Miss Perry looked more puzzled than ever. "What walls? Gregory, do you know what she means?"

He told her, "She means the walls in back of my house. I made a garden there—out of chalk."

"Out of *chalk*?" said Miss Perry.

"That's my garden," he said. "That's the one I talked about."

"I see." Miss Perry came back and picked up the leather case. "This is yours, Ivy," she said. "It's part of your prize, and your name is on it. But if Gregory's pictures are as good as you say, I can see why you want him to have a prize too." She put the case down on Ivy's desk.

The bell rang. School began.

At noon Miss Perry said to Gregory, "I'd like to see these walls of yours. And I'm sure Miss Cartright would too. When may we see them?"

"Anytime," he said.

"Today after school?" she asked.

"Yes," he said.

They walked home with him after school, Miss Perry and Miss Cartright. He opened the gate for them.

Miss Perry said, "Oh!"

Miss Cartright said, "It really *is* a garden!"

They looked at the walls and talked to each other. They sounded excited.

"The pictures he did in art were nice, but nothing like this!" said Miss Cartright. "I heard him say a piece of paper wasn't big enough. I think he needed a whole wall!"

Miss Perry asked him, "Where did you get the idea for this?"

"From Mr. Hiller," he said.

"I want him to see it," said Miss Perry.

Mr. Hiller came to see the garden.

"I'd like a picture of this," he said. "A big picture to put up in the nursery. May I bring my camera over tomorrow?"

"Yes," said Gregory.

On the way out Mr. Hiller met Daddy. Daddy had just come home from work.

"Are you this boy's father?" asked Mr. Hiller.

"I am," said Daddy.

"I just saw Gregory's garden," said Mr. Hiller. "You must be proud."

"Proud?" said Daddy.

"Yes, proud," said Mr. Hiller, and he left.

Mother came out. "Who was that?"

"I don't know," said Daddy, "but I think we'd better see what is behind our house."

They went out into the burned building. Gregory went with them.

Mother looked at the walls. "Oh, Gregory!"

"We'll have to get new clothes," said Daddy.

"New clothes?" asked Mother.

"Yes," said Daddy, "because our son is going to be famous and everybody will be looking at us."

Mother called Uncle Max, and he came out. He looked at the garden for a while. "First he was the Paintbrush Kid," he said. "Now he's the Chalk Box Kid."

It sounded like a joke, but Uncle Max wasn't laughing. And that night, when Gregory went to bed, he saw his old pictures on the wall.

"Where are your posters?" he asked his uncle.

"I took them down," said Uncle Max.

Things were different at school. Everyone he met was friendly. Even Vance was friendly. "There's a picture of your garden down at the nursery," he said. "Why don't you go see it?"

But the best thing of all happened one evening after school. Gregory was making a place for his fountain when Ivy came to the gate and looked in. A little boy was with her.

"This is my brother Richard," she said. "I brought him to see."

Gregory had piled up bricks and made places to sit. The three of them sat on the bricks in front of the walls.

Ivy whispered to her brother, "This isn't like our garden, Richard. This is different. This is somebody else's garden."

"I see it," said the little boy.

Gregory told Ivy, "I'm putting in a fountain. Do you want to help me?"

"I don't know," she whispered. "I might."

Then they were quiet, and they sat there for a long time.

About the Author

CLYDE ROBERT BULLA is an outstanding children's book author, with more than sixty books and many awards to his credit. About *The Chalk Box Kid* he writes, "When I was young, I sometimes found it hard to cope in new surroundings, and I was apt to get off on the wrong foot. This is the story of a boy who got off on the wrong foot in a new school and how he tried to cope. I gave Gregory something I've always wished for: a big, blank wall that I could cover with my own drawings."

Clyde Robert Bulla grew up in King City, Missouri, and now lives in Los Angeles, California.

About the Illustrator

THOMAS B. ALLEN has illustrated several books for children, including *Blackberries in the Dark, In Coal Country,* and *The Secret Garden.* He was born in Nashville, Tennessee, and now lives in Lawrence, Kansas, where he is Hallmark Distinguished Professor in the Department of Design at the University of Kansas.